Geronimo Stilton

MY NAME IS STILTON, GERONIMO STILTON

Scholastic Inc.

New York   Toronto   London   Auckland   Sydney

Mexico City   New Delhi   Hong Kong   Buenos Aires

ISBN 0-439-69142-7

Copyright © 2000 by Edizioni Piemme S.p.A., Via del Carmine 5, 15033 Casale Monferrato (AL), Italia.
English translation © 2005 by Edizioni Piemme S.p.A.

Stilton is the name of a famous English cheese. It is a registered trademark of the Stilton Cheese Makers' Association. For more information, go to www.stiltoncheese.com.

Text by Geronimo Stilton
Original title: *Il mio nome è Stilton, Geronimo Stilton*
Cover by Larry Keys
Illustrations from ideas by Larry Keys; drawn by Raterto Rattonchi
Graphics by Merenguita Gingermouse

Special thanks to Tracey West
Interior design by Kay Petronio

12 11 10 9 8 7 6 5   6 7 8 9 10/0

Printed in the U.S.A.   23
First printing, May 2005

Dear mouse friends,
Welcome to the world of

Geronimo Stilton

The Editorial Staff of
The Rodent's Gazette

1. Linda Thinslice
2. Sweetie Cheesetriangle
3. Ratella Redfur
4. Soya Mousehao
5. Cheesita de la Pampa
6. Coco Chocamouse
7. Mouseanna Mousetti
8. Patty Plumprat
9. Tina Spicytail
10. William Shortpaws
11. Valerie Vole
12. Trap Stilton
13. Dolly Fastpaws
14. Zeppola Zap
15. Merenguita Gingermouse
16. Shorty Tao
17. Baby Tao
18. Gigi Gogo
19. Teddy von Muffler
20. Thea Stilton
21. Erronea Misprint
22. Pinky Pick
23. Ya-ya O'Cheddar
24. Ratsy O'Shea
25. Geronimo Stilton
26. Benjamin Stilton
27. Briette Finerat
28. Raclette Finerat
29. Mousella MacMouser
30. Kreamy O'Cheddar
31. Blasco Tabasco
32. Toffie Sugarsweet
33. Tylerat Truemouse
34. Larry Keys
35. Michael Mouse

Geronimo Stilton
A learned and brainy
mouse; editor of
The Rodent's Gazette

Thea Stilton
Geronimo's sister and
special correspondent at
The Rodent's Gazette

Trap Stilton
An awful joker;
Geronimo's cousin and
owner of the store
Cheap Junk for Less

Benjamin Stilton
A sweet and loving
nine-year-old mouse;
Geronimo's favorite
nephew

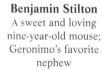

MY NAME IS STILTON

My name is Stilton, Geronimo Stilton.

I like to think of myself as a very normal mouse.

I have a pretty normal job. I am the publisher of *The Rodent's Gazette*. It is the most popular newspaper in New Mouse City.

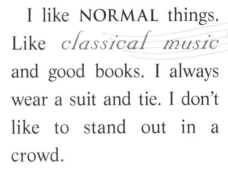

I like **NORMAL** things. Like *classical music* and good books. I always wear a suit and tie. I don't like to stand out in a crowd.

When I order a pizza, I take it plain. No anchovies,

please! I don't like **loud rock music.**
I don't wear clothes with polka dots or stripes
or **bright colors**. And I
will take a slice of bland American cheese
over a chunk of jalapeño hot-pepper cheese
any day.

As you can see, I like my life to be calm
and peaceful. I know some people
might think I'm plain, or even
boring. That may be true. But
that is how I like it!

So why am I telling you all
of this?

Let me explain.........

TOO MUCH
WORK

Things were very busy at the newspaper office. I was working so hard that I had not had time to get my fur clipped in months! Something had to be done.

Then I had a great idea. I decided to hire an assistant. I placed an ad in the paper, and hundreds of mice sent in their résumés.

I read them all. One stood out from the rest.

"This is exactly the mouse I am looking for!" I cried.

I called my secretary, Mousella. She came into my office.

"Mousella, please draw up a contract right

away!" I said. "I have found the perfect assistant. It says here her name is Pinky Pick. She is young and smart. She has excellent **COMPUTER** skills. And she is an expert on the latest trends. That is just what we need! A **TRENDY** mouse!"

Mousella frowned. "Don't you want to bring her in for an interview first?" she asked.

I did not want to wait. Pinky Pick sounded perfect! "There is no need for that," I said.

"I have years of experience as a newspaper editor. I just need to look a rodent in the snout to know if he or she will do a good job or not. I CAN FEEL IT IN MY WHISKERS! She is going to be great."

"Of course," Mousella said. "But, er, are you sure . . ."

"My whiskers never lie!" I snapped. I did not want to argue. I was so sure I was right!

A MOUSE IN PLATFORM SNEAKERS

The next day, I woke up before sunrise. I had to get to the office early to **CATCH UP** with my work. I brushed my teeth with cheddar toothpaste. Then I got dressed and ran downstairs.

My driver was waiting for me. I got into my *car*, and we drove through the empty streets of New Mouse City. At six in the morning, everything was peaceful and quiet. Just how I like it.

The driver pulled up in front of 17 Swiss Cheese Center. I walked

in the building and headed down a **long** hallway covered with cheese-yellow wallpaper. Then I opened the door to my office. Stacks of paper COVERED the floor and desk.

"Cheese niblets, this is a lot of work!" I squeaked. "Thank goodness, my new assistant will be here today."

I closed the door behind me and went to work. At eleven

o'clock, Mousella knocked on my door. She stepped into my office.

"Mr. Stilton, the new assistant is here," she said. "But I think you should see her before she $signs$ the contract."

"Yes, yes, the contract," I said. I was so busy with work, I was not really listening to Mousella.

"But, Mr. Stilton, I really think you should see her," Mousella insisted.

"I am very BUSY!" I squeaked. "I do not need to see her. Please take care of it for me!"

Mousella looked amazed. "As you wish, Mr. Stilton," she said. "I will get her to sign the contract. But you should know that she has a request. She would like three months' pay in advance. She says she has offers from other newspapers. I told her that a serious mouse like you would never agree to that. But it is up to you, of course."

"Yes, yes, *whatever*," I said. Once again, I wasn't really listening.

Mousella left, shaking her head. I thought I saw her *smile slyly* as she closed the door.

"That is strange," I muttered. Then I went back to work.

A minute later, there was another knock on the door.

"I said, I am very busy!"

I cried, not looking up from my work. The door opened anyway. A young female mouse stood there. She looked like she was about fourteen years old. She had gray fur and a POINTED snout.

But it was her outfit that really got my attention. The first thing I noticed was her shoes. **I COULD NOT BELIEVE MY EYES!**

Her shoes were enormouse. They were shocking pink high-top sneakers with high, see-through platform soles. Inside the platforms, pink plastic fish swam in water. A bright light flashed on and off, illuminating the fish.

The rest of her outfit was just as **RiDiCULOUS**. She wore bright green leggings under a large yellow sweatshirt. Swiss cheese holes dotted her shirt.

And that wasn't all. She had a clear plastic

backpack on her back. A diary covered in **FAKE CAT FUR** dangled from the backpack strap. It was shocking pink, just like her shoes. Papers and photos stuck out from the pages. It was clamped shut with a **BIG LOCK** shaped like a cat's head.

I had never seen anything like it. Her clothes were so bright, I wished I was wearing sunglasses!

*Pink plastic fish were swimming
inside her platform sneakers.*

My Name Is Pick

"My name is **PICK!**" the brightly dressed mouse yelled.

"That's nice, little girl," I said, going back to my work. "My name is *Stilton, Geronimo Stilton.* If you are looking for the office of *Mini Mouse* magazine, the publication for young mouselets, you're in the wrong place."

"I am *not* looking for *Mini Mouse* magazine," she said. "I told you. My name is **PICK!**"

The name sounded familiar. Then I remembered. Pinky Pick was the name of my new assistant.

"Are you looking for your mother?" I asked. "Because I am waiting for her, too. She is going to start working for me today."

The little mouse leaned over my desk. Her eyes glittered.

"No, *I* am going to start working for you today," she said. "My name is **PINKY PICK**. I am your new assistant. Get it, Boss?"

Nobody had ever called me boss before.

I didn't like it.

Not one bit!

WHAT'S THE PROBLEM, BOSS?

Platform sneakers? Boss? My new assistant? My head was spinning faster than the Screamin' Rat Roller Coaster at the amousement park.

"**YOU . . . YOU are MY new assistant?**" I stammered. It could not be true.

"That's right!" she said. She leaned back and folded her arms.

"But you're so young!" I squeaked.

"For your information, I am already *fourteen*," she said calmly.

I shook my snout. "That is too young to work at a newspaper."

"That's what you think," she said. She held up one shocking-pink foot. "I wear size **twelve** shoes. I bet my paws are bigger than anyone's on your staff. Bigger than yours, even."

"I don't care what your shoe size is," I replied. "When I was your age, I was playing with my **TEDDY MOUSE**. Not working on a newspaper."

Pinky Pick shrugged. "It's not my fault you didn't have any goals back then."

Cheese nips! This little mouse was starting to get on my nerves.

"Listen, young lady," I said. "I need a true professional to be my assistant. Not a little mouselet like you. Now, please run along."

But Pinky Pick did not leave. Instead, she

sat down in the chair in front of my desk.

"So why did you hire me?" she asked softly.

"Hire you?" I cried. "Why would I hire someone like you? That's ridiculous!"

Pinky smiled. She pulled a piece of paper out of her backpack and WAVED it in front of my snout. It was a contract made out to Pinky Pick. And there was my signature, *Geronimo Stilton*, right on the bottom!

"You see, Boss?" Pinky said. "You are so busy, you don't even know what you are signing. That is why you need a good assistant like me."

"Mousella!" I screamed. My secretary scurried into the office. She had a **LITTLE SMIRK** on her face.

"Yes, Mr. Stilton?" she asked.

I grabbed the contract from Pinky Pick.

"Why did you let me sign this?" I asked. "You should have told me she was only *fourteen*."

"Why, Mr. Stilton, I tried to warn you," Mousella said in a smooth voice. "But you told me your whiskers never lie. And that you were very busy. And . . ."

"Yes, yes," I moaned. I *had* said all of those things. "Well, we will just have to start again. Put another ad in the newspaper."

Pinky Pick jumped up. She unclipped her big diary and **SLAMMED** it on my desk.

"Let me help you out, Boss," she said. "Just tell me what you need. What's your problem?"

I sighed. Of course, I could not take this little

I am looking for information on a very rare cheese.

mouse seriously. But I *did* have a problem.

"I am sure you can't help me," I said. "I have to find information on a very rare cheese for an article I am writing. I don't even know what it's called. It is made in a small village in the **Fossil Forest**. I need to know how it is made. And how much it costs."

Pinky Pick grinned. "Leave it to me, Boss," she said. "I can find anything on the **Net**. I'm a regular cheese whiz when it comes to the computer."

She sat down in front of the **COMPUTER** and grabbed the mouse. I didn't try to stop her. Something told me she wouldn't take no for an answer!

AN IMPOSSIBLE INTERVIEW

I could not believe it. Half an hour later, Pinky Pick was done.

"Here you are," she said. "The cheese is called **MEGACHEESE**. It comes from the village of Little Cheeseville. They only make seven whole cheeses a year," she said. "That is because it takes three thousand gallons of milk to make one pound of cheese! It's **VERY nutritious**. And very expensive."

"How did you do it?" I asked. I was impressed.

She shrugged. "*No sweat*," she said.

"Anyone could do it."

"But I searched for days, and I couldn't find it," I said.

"I'm sure you would have found it . . . someday," Pinky said. Her eyes TWINKLED.

"Maybe I could use your help after all," I muttered. "Just for small jobs, of course."

"Give me another problem!" Pinky shouted. "I'm ready to go!"

I covered my ears. "Calm down!" I cried. "Your voice is LOUDER than your outfit."

I looked through my notes. "Here is something," I said. "Fuzzy Fuzzborn is in town. The ROCK singer. Every reporter in town wants to interview him."

I am not a big fan of Fuzzy Fuzzborn's. As I said before, I don't like loud rock music. But he is one of the most popular mice on Mouse

Island. An interview with Fuzzy would be great for *The Rodent's Gazette*. There was only one problem.

"Fuzzy never gives interviews," I told Pinky. "He is a pretty cranky rat. Not even *you* could handle this one. No one can! I will find something else."

But Pinky had already strapped on her IN-LINE SKATES. She pushed off my desk and zoomed toward the door.

"ONE INTERVIEW, COMING UP!" she cried.

I tried to jump out of the way. But there was no time.

That little mouse skated right over my tail!

TRICKS OF THE TRADE

Pinky skated in two hours later. "Here's your interview, Boss," she said. "I even took pictures of him!"

I was shocked. **"But Fuzzy Fuzzborn never gives interviews. To anyone!"** I squeaked. **"How did you do it?"**

Pinky sat down. She plopped her big platform sneakers on my desk.

"Take your fishy footwear off my desk!" I cried.

"All right, all right," Pinky said, lowering her paws. "Don't get your fur frazzled, Boss. Don't you want to read the interview?"

To tell the truth, I wanted to read the interview very badly. An interview with Fuzzy

Pinky took a signed photo of Fuzzy out of her backpack.

Fuzzborn! What a SCOOP! But I didn't want Pinky Pick to see how EXCITED I was. She might get the wrong idea. Like that I actually wanted her to be my assistant.

Pinky winked at me. "Let me tell you all about it, *Uncle* Geronimo," she said.

"Uncle? How dare you call me that!" I shrieked.

"OK," said Pinky. "How about Pops?"

"You can't call me Pops, either!" I said. "Call me Mr. Stilton. I am your boss, after all."

As soon as I'd uttered the word *boss*, I realized my mistake. But it was too late.

"Aha!" Pinky said. "If you are my boss, that means I am your new assistant. Right?"

"Fine, fine!" I said. THE LITTLE MOUSE HAD FINALLY WORN ME DOWN. "Just show me the interview, please!"

At that moment, my sister, Thea, ran into the office. Thea is a special correspondent for *The Rodent's Gazette*. She knows everything that happens in New Mouse City.

Thea ran up to Pinky and shook her paw. "GOOD job, kid!" my sister said. "I heard about the interview with Fuzzy. How did you do it?"

Pinky grinned. "Check this out," she said. She took a large photo of Fuzzy Fuzzborn out of her backpack. Fuzzy had signed it:

To Pinky Pick, the most adorable, fabumouse, smartest mouse on Mouse Island.

"This is how I did it," Pinky said. "I wrote him a letter. It went like this:

Dear Fuzzy,

I am your biggest fan! I know all of your songs by heart.

I have covered the walls in my room with your pictures.

when I grow up, I want to be just like you!

"Then I added some details," Pinky went on. "I said I had a mean boss who made me work day and night for no pay. I told him you forced me to interview him or you would fire me."

I couldn't believe it. Such lies! I had not forced Pinky to do anything. She was the one who forced herself on me!

"Well, I never—" I began. But the phone RANG before I could finish. I picked it up.

"Hello. Is this Stilton, Geronimo Stilton?" the caller asked.

I recognized the voice right away. It was

Fuzzy Fuzzborn!

"Yes, I am Geronimo Stilton," I said. I was EXCITED. "I am so pleased you did an interview for our paper, Mr. Fuzzborn."

"I only did it to help out that sweet little mouse who works for you!" Fuzzy snapped. "Shame on you! How dare you make her work day and night! What kind of a terrible boss are you? She is just a little mouselet!"

I started to tell him the truth, but Pinky slapped her PAW over my mouth.

"Oh, my assistant has a great imagination," I managed to mumble. "I am sure she was stretching the truth a bit."

But Fuzzy did not believe me.

"Shame on you, Stilton!" he squeaked.

"SHAME ON YOU!"

How Embarrassing!

"You stink worse than a hunk of rotten cheese, Stilton!"

Fuzzy was shouting.

How embarrassing!

Fuzzy Fuzzborn was one of the most famouse rats on Mouse Island. And he thought I was a first-class creep! What if he started spreading Pinky's story around? My reputation would be ruined. And it was all Pinky's fault.

That's it, I decided. I can't have this meddling mouse as my assistant.

BEFORE I COULD SAY ANYTHING, Pinky pressed the speaker button on my phone. Fuzzy's voice rang out through the office.

"And another thing, Stilton," Fuzzy said. "That little assistant of yours is a genius! Her interview was brilliant. She really understands me and my music. I am thinking of letting her write my biography."

All thoughts of firing Pinky left my brain. Fuzzy Fuzzborn's biography? That was an even bigger SCOOp than the interview!

Pinky Pick grinned. She sat down and put her big shoes on my desk.

I motioned for her to move her paws.

She didn't. Instead, she made a face at me!

THE DAILY RAT

I started thinking about firing Pinky again. Biography or not, she was just too much!

Fuzzy was still talking. "You are lucky to have an assistant like **PINKY PICK**, Stilton," he said. "I am sure she could teach you a thing or two. You'd better keep her happy or you might lose her!"

"Of course, Fuzzy. Of course," I said. But inside I was still fuming.

Fuzzy finally hung up. Pinky jumped out of her seat.

"I think it's time for a raise, Boss!" she shouted.

My furry face flushed red. "**Raise!**" I shrieked. "**BUT I JUST HIRED YOU!**"

Pinky winked at me. "Too bad. I guess I

could always go work for the competition."

I turned as PALE as a piece of mozzarella. *The Daily Rat* was my biggest competition in New Mouse City. If Pinky worked there, *they* would get the Fuzzy Fuzzborn interview. And the biography. I gulped.

"Now, don't be hasty, Pinky," I said. "Aren't you happy here at *The Rodent's Gazette* with your **uncle Gerry**?"

Pinky smiled. "Here's the deal," she said, slapping her paws on my desk. "I want a huge . . . no, a mega-huge bonus each year.

I love to travel, so I also need three months of paid vacation. And I want all my expenses paid, including my clothes. I need to keep up with the latest trends." She pointed to her **BAGGY** sweatshirt.

"Well, that's all very *expensive*," I said.

Pinky sat down and folded her arms behind her head. "I understand, Boss. If you don't like the deal, I can always go somewhere else. I already have an idea for Fuzzborn's biography."

Pinky's gaze moved to the top of my desk. A copy of *The Daily Rat* stared up at us.

I would not let them **scoop** me with the Fuzzy Fuzzborn story. I could not let that happen!

"Whatever you want, Pinky," I said. "Whatever you want!"

THE ASSISTANT'S ASSISTANT

So it was all settled. Pinky Pick was my new assistant. *The Rodent's Gazette* was going to get the Fuzzy Fuzzborn interview and biography. I arrived at my office early the next morning, ready for a calm and peaceful day.

But I had not even finished my cheese pastry when Pinky Pick burst through my door.

"I have NEWS, Boss!" she squeaked.

"NEWS about Fuzzy?" I asked hopefully.

"No, there is more NEWS," she said. "Come on, ask me what it is."

"All right, Pinky," I said. "What is it?"

Pinky moved to one side. "Ta-da!" she shouted.

A small female mouse stepped out from

behind Pinky. She looked like she was about fourteen, too.

"**WHO ARE YOU?**" I asked.

"My name is **Merry Melody**," she said shyly.

"Shouldn't you be in school?" I asked.

Pinky laughed. "It's **CHRISTMAS** vacation! There is no school. By the way, this is Merry—my new assistant!"

"Assistant!" I shouted. "Who said you were allowed to have an assistant?"

Pinky did not answer. Instead, she unhooked the **big diary** from her backpack. She **OPENED** it up to reveal a built-in CALCULATOR.

"Hmm," she said, punching in numbers. "With Merry's help, I could write Fuzzy's biography faster. I could do it in one month instead of two!"

A Cheese-scented Diary

Pinky had my attention. Of course, it was ridiculous for an assistant to have an assistant. But if Fuzzy's biography could get done faster that way . . .

"All right," I said. "But how much will your assistant cost me?"

Pinky whispered a number in my ear.

"HOLEY CHEESE!" I cried in HORROR. "I could buy a lifetime supply of cheddar with that kind of money!"

Then Pinky whispered something else in my ear.

"WHAT?" I asked. "How much did *The Daily Rat* offer you?"

I had no choice. I had to hire Merry or lose Pinky—and Fuzzy Fuzzborn—to *The Daily Rat.*

The morning had been much too

exciting for me. I wanted to forget about Pinky Pick—just for a little while. So later that day, I called a meeting of my staff at the publishing house.

I asked my sales manager for a report. "We need to make new products," Shif T. Paws said. "Something MODERN. Something exciting. Something for today's youth."

From behind me, a small voice said, "No problem! I have lots of ideas!"

I cringed. Pinky Pick ran into the room, carrying a stack of papers.

"How about a diary with cheese-scented pages? A series of biographies on rock singers? Or a backpack on wheels?" she asked. "And here's the best idea of all. We should publish a magazine for young mice. We can call it Fur Kids Only. And I think the right rodent for the job is . . . me!"

How Could You?

My staff gobbled up Pinky's IDEAS like hungry rats at an all-you-can-eat cheese bar. I had to admit, her ideas were all pretty good.

We started production on everything. The cheese-scented diary. The magazine. It all sold like crazy.

I started to think that hiring Pinky Pick was not such a bad idea after all.

Sure, she is loud. And pushy. And wears ridiculous clothes, I told myself. *But she knows how to make money for this company!*

My mouse-gray walls had been splattered with paint!

So I had a smile on my snout as I walked into my building a few days later. I opened my office door and stepped inside.

For a second, I thought I had gone through the wrong door. The room looked like Pinky's office.

But then I saw my desk, my papers, my cheese-shaped paperweight. . . .

"CHEESE NIBLETS!" I shrieked. "Pinky, what have you done?"

My lovely mouse-gray walls had been splattered with paint. Lines, squiggles, and doodles in bright colors stared back at me. Red, blue, yellow, green, purple, and pink. Shocking pink, of course!

Pinky ran into the room, waving a spray can. "How do you like it, Boss?" she asked. "I did it for free. Because I like you!"

"If you really liked me, you would have left

my office alone!" I WAILED.

Just then, Merry flung open the door. She rushed into the room.

The door slaMMed into my snout.

I fell against the coat stand. The stand fell on my head.

I stumbled. One PAW landed in the umbrella stand. The other paw landed on top of the computer plug.

A SHOCK of electricity raced through me.

"Yeeow!" I shrieked. My fur stood on end.

I broke away from the plug and slammed into Pinky. Her spray can went off, and orange paint sprayed my snout.

"**Heeeelp!**" I screamed.

Mousella and the rest of the staff came running. They all stared at me.

Finally, my art director, Tylerat Truemouse, spoke up.

"Mr. Stilton, why are you dressed up like a **punk** rocker?" he asked.

HAPPY BIRTHDAY, STILTON!

It took me all day to wash the orange paint out of my fur. I went home that night in a **bad mood**.

Not only was my office ruined, but it was M Y B I R T H D A Y ! And nobody had remembered.

Now, I don't like to make a big deal of my birthday. A nice, quiet celebration is just fine. But I had not even received a single phone call. Not even from my aunt Sweetfur.

Aunt Sweetfur always sends me a birthday card. Of course, she still treats me like I am five years old. Last year's card had a picture of a tiny mouse holding a balloon. It said,

"To my sweet little cheeselet!"
It's the thought that counts.

I was in no hurry to get back to my empty mouse hole. So I walked home.

First I passed the newsstand. Copies of **Pinky's new magazine** were stacked on every shelf.

Then I passed the bookstore. Pinky's **cheese-scented** diary filled the window display.

Normally, the store stacked *my* bestselling books in their window. But it seemed they had **forgotten** about me. Just like everyone else. I sighed.

A few minutes later, I slumped up the stairs of my building. I unlocked my door and pushed it open.

Suddenly, the lights came on.

"HAPPY BIRTHDAY!"

"Cheesecake!" I squeaked. I JUMPED back. I hate surprises!

About a hundred mice filled my house! They all began to sing:

May you have a happy day.
Raise your snout and shout, "Hooray!"
Now it's time to celebrate,
Because your assistant is really great!

Your assistant is really great? What kind of birthday song was that?

Suddenly, I understood.

The crowd parted. Pinky Pick stood in the **center** of the room. She was with Thea, my cousin Trap, and my nephew Benjamin.

"Aha!" I cried. Pinky was behind this party. And I knew that could *not* be good!

Thea grabbed me. "Hey, Germeister," she said. "This party was a great idea! And it's all thanks to Pinky."

Thea gave Pinky a hug. Then it hit me.

Thea and Pinky are a lot alike! They are both loud. And they both like to stir up trouble.

I moaned. Somehow I knew **MY LIFE WOULD NEVER BE CALM AND PEACEFUL** again. I grabbed a mozzarella stick from the snack table and began to munch on it to calm my nerves.

Suddenly, I felt a slap on my back. I nearly choked on my mozzarella!

I turned around. It was my cousin Trap, of course.

"It's about time YOU HAD A PARTY, Gerry Berry," he said. "That assistant of yours is good for you. I love your new office. That old gray mouse hole of yours was so depressing."

"But I *liked* my gray mouse hole!" I protested.

"And you were always such a **penny-pincher**," Trap went on. "I'm glad to see

you're living it up a bit. *Caviar, truffles, champagne, imported cheese . . .*"

I followed Trap's gaze across the room. Someone had set up a huge table piled with expensive food.

I had a bad feeling. I started to look around. Benjamin, my dear little nephew, pulled my sleeve.

"Uncle Geronimo, isn't Pinky pretty?" he

squeaked. "Will you please introduce me?"

But I ignored him. I was too busy noticing other, bigger changes in my house.

Someone had set up huge arrangements of *EXPENSIVE FLOWERS*. A shocking pink *silk carpet* lined my hallway. And each guest was carrying a little gift: a solid PLATINUM cheese holder with a diamond on the lid!

I had that feeling again.

This could *not* be good!

SNAP FLASHFUR

I was right. Things only got WORSE.

To start with, the sound of loud music suddenly filled my living room. I looked in the corner and saw that the famous rock band Rat Attack was pounding away on their guitars.

I also saw a mouse with long, dark fur carrying a camera. He was talking to guests and taking pictures. I would know that snout anywhere. It was SNAPFLASHFUR, the famous photographer. He only took pictures of the biggest celebrities.

FLASH!
FLASH!
FLASH!

"What is he doing here?" I asked.

"Isn't it wonderful?" Thea said, beaming. She loves to rub elbows with important mice. "We hired only the best for

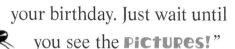

your birthday. Just wait until you see the **PICTURES!**"

Snap walked up to me. "**MY DEAR MR. STILTON!** Look at these wonderful photos I took of you. You didn't even notice I was doing it. I get the best pictures that way."

I looked at the photos. One showed just my paw. The other was my body without a head. My nephew Benjamin takes better photos than that!

But Thea loved them. *"Brilliant!"* she said, clapping her paws together. "Snap, you are a *genius*. Nobody takes photos like you do!"

"Who would want to?" I muttered.

But Snap's photos were the least of my worries. I had to ask Thea a question. And I was not sure I wanted the answer.

"Who is **paying** for all of this?" I asked nervously.

WHAT A
WONDERFUL IDEA!

Thea burst out laughing. "Why, you are paying, of course! Pinky organized everything. Wasn't that sweet of her? She said she would do it for free because you are such a good boss."

"Oh, dear," I said. I suddenly felt queasy.

"But the best is yet to come," Thea went on. "In a few minutes, the *great poet* Walt Whitmouse will read a poem in your honor. He charged a lot of money to write it, but it's worth every penny. After that, a thousand BALLOONS will be released into the sky. Then there are the fireworks. Don't worry about those. We hired four of the best fireworks experts around to light them.

They're waiting on the roof right now."

Balloons? Fireworks? Expensive poetry? The room started to swim before my eyes.

But there was more.

"And wait until you see your **BIRTHDAY CAKE**," Thea said. "Pinky and I came up with this idea together. We're so much alike, aren't we? Anyway, the cake has ten layers.

Each layer is a foot high, with cream cheese frosting and **CANDIED CHERRIES**. On the very top is a winged mouse made of Parmesan cheese."

A ten-foot cake? I started to groan.

"We had such a hard time trying to get someone to bake it for us," Thea continued. "But Pinky and I said only the *best* for our Geronimo! So the Blue Ribbon Bakery agreed to stay CLOSED for a week so they could spend all their time baking your cake. It took twenty bakers working day and night to finish it!"

I sat down on the couch. My head was spinning. I could barely breathe. In my head, I started adding up what everything would **cost** . . . the caviar . . . the cake . . . the fireworks . . . the band . . . the terrible photos. . . .

I ended up with a very large number with

a lot of zeroes on the end.

I fainted.

I came to when Trap dumped the contents of an ice bucket on my head.

"**NOOOOO!**" I moaned. "**THIS CAN'T BE HAPPENING!**"

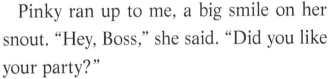

Pinky ran up to me, a big smile on her snout. "Hey, Boss," she said. "Did you like your party?"

"I can honestly say that this is a birthday I will never forget," I grumbled. I stood up, brushing ice cubes off my fur.

"Did you tell him yet?" Thea asked Pinky.

I got a bad feeling again. "Tell me what?" I asked.

"Gerrykins, Pinky had a brilliant idea," Thea said. "We are all going on a trip to the **NORTH POLE!**"

"The North Pole!" I squeaked. "Why on earth would I want to go there? It is freezing cold. And there are no cheese shops there."

"Pinky made a deal with **MouseTV**," Thea explained. "We are going to celebrate New Year's Eve at the North Pole. The TV station is going to film it. Isn't that great?"

I was speechless.

"Get a good night's sleep, Boss," Pinky said. "We leave first thing in the morning."

THE NORTH POLE?

TOMORROW MORNING?

I fainted again!

RISE AND SHINE!

I did not sleep well that night. I kept having nightmares about BEING OUTSIDE in the freezing North Pole. I felt cold . . . so cold . . .

I woke up to find that Trap had dumped another ice bucket on me! My cousin stood there with Benjamin, Merry, and, of course, Pinky.

"Rise and shine, Cousinkins," Trap said. "It's time to leave!"

I jumped out of bed. Ice cubes slid to the floor.

"You did not have to wake me up like that," I grumbled. "Besides, I am not going to THE NORTH POLE!"

Pinky shoved a pile of clothes into my paws. There was a pair of boots lined with fake CAT FUR, a parka, earmuffs, gloves, and other cold-weather gear. Everything was Pinky's favorite color, of course—shocking pink!

"I will not wear this stuff!" I protested. "Anyway, where is Thea? Isn't she a part of this?"

Suddenly, I heard a very loud noise outside. I HAD another BAD FEELING. I ran up to the roof. Trap and the others scurried behind me.

There, hovering in the sky, was a helicopter! Thea leaned out the window and waved. Her violet eyes were gleaming!

"All aboard!" she cried.

"Absolutely not!" I squeaked. "I would rather give up cheese than get on that helicopter! I am not going and I mean it! Or my name is not GERONIMO STILTON!

Thea waved at us from the helicopter.

SOMEDAY YOU WILL THANK ME

Ten minutes later, I was sitting in the helicopter.

I had no choice but to put on the shocking pink parka that Pinky had given me. Thank goodness SNAPFLASHFUR wasn't around to take a picture!

I was tired, dressed in pink, and heading for the NORTH POLE. Definitely not a happy mouse. But Pinky was smiling brightly.

"Just wait, Boss," she said. "There is a **fabumouse** party waiting for us at the North Pole. We'll have the best New Year's Eve ever. And we'll be on every TV set in Mouse Island!"

"How could you do this?" I wailed.

"I did it for you, Boss," Pinky said. "I know you love attention. There is nothing better than being on TV! Believe me, someday you will thank me for this."

"Cats will eat cheese before I thank you for this," I mumbled.

I was miserable. The trip took hours and hours. I thought it would never end. My stomach always gets queasy when I fly. Every time I looked out the window, I GOT DIZZY.

My sister looked like she was having the time of her life. She piloted the helicopter like a real pro.

When we finally came to the NORTH POLE, my whiskers began to tremble. I just knew something was going to go wrong!

NORTH POLE, HERE WE COME!

"Get ready to land!" Thea shouted.

Thea steered the helicopter so it pointed down. Right below us, I saw an enormouse ship. As we got closer, I saw it was an **icebreaker**. It pushed its way through the frozen seas.

"Here we are!" Thea yelled. She aimed the helicopter at the ship's wide deck. A cold wind blew across the water, but we landed

safely. When the helicopter blades stopped spinning, we walked onto the deck.

A rat in a captain's uniform greeted us. "YOU MUST BE STILTON, GERONIMO STILTON," he said in a crisp voice. "I AM NELSON, CAPTAIN OCEANUS NELSON. It is a pleasure to meet you."

I shook his paw. Then he turned to my sister, Thea. His whiskers began to quiver.

"What a BEAUTIFUL LANDING!" he gushed. He took her paw and kissed it. "You should have joined the navy, my dear lady. They could use a talented and lovely rat like you!"

I groaned quietly. Everywhere Thea went, rats tripped over their tails to get her attention. It looked like Captain Nelson was no different!

Pinky stepped forward. She took out her diary and began to flip through the pages. "Let's get busy, crew!" she shouted. "New Year's Eve is the day after tomorrow."

The captain took his eyes off Thea and turned to me with a serious look.

"MY SHIPPING COMPANY TOLD ME YOU NEEDED THIS SHIP FOR AN IMPORTANT MISSION," he said. **"EXACTLY WHAT KIND OF MISSION IS IT?"**

"Oh, just wait and see," Thea piped up. "It's going to be fun."

"Yes, fun," Pinky agreed. But she didn't give any details, either.

Captain Nelson didn't seem to like that.

He pulled me aside.

"**LISTEN HERE, STILTON**," he said. "**I HAVE TWO VERY IMPORTANT QUESTIONS FOR YOU. ONE: WHAT KIND OF MISSION ARE YOU PLANNING? AND TWO: DOES YOUR SISTER HAVE A BOYFRIEND?**"

I sighed. I might as well tell Captain Nelson the truth. "I think the special mission is some kind of **party**," I said.

Captain Nelson raised his furry eyebrows in surprise. "**A PARTY? THIS IS A REAL SHIP! YOU CANNOT HAVE A PARTY HERE!**" he squeaked.

I decided to change the subject. "As for my sister," I said, "she does not have a boyfriend. *IN FACT*, I am sure she would love to go to the party with you!"

A Spooky Shape
in the Fog

Captain Nelson and I were interrupted by the sound of excited squeaks.

Pinky and Thea were exploring the ship.

"We should have the party in here," Thea was saying, walking around the large galley.

"Right," said Pinky. She began pointing around the ship. "The food tables will be here. We'll need a lot, because I'm expecting about five hundred guests. Maybe a thousand, even."

Then Pinky walked over to a door with a plate that read, CAPTAIN NELSON'S OFFICE. "Perfect!" she said. "The rock band can go in here!"

Captain Nelson turned pale. I felt sorry

for him. I knew just how he felt!

I decided to leave Pinky and Thea to their plans. I walked up on deck.

The air was bitter cold. I was glad to be wearing my parka, even if it was pink. I leaned over the railing and gazed out across the water.

White foam capped the waves like fluffy whiskers. It was rather *beautiful.* The sun was setting, streaking the sky a lovely shade of cheddar gold. Maybe this trip would not be so bad after all!

Then things suddenly grew dark. The ship had sailed into a misty gray *fog.*

Boooo-eeeeee. The ship's fog signal rang out in the night. But then something caught my eye.

There was a big, dark shape looming in front of us in the fog.

Was I seeing THINGS?

I cleaned my glasses so I could see better. Then I put them on again.

The shape was still there. Right in front of the ship. It was getting closer.

I gulped. It looked just like . . .

"An iceberg!" I squeaked.

We were about to crash into an enormouse

iceberg! I had to do something.

"**HELP!**" I screamed. "Help!"

I ran around the deck, trying to find my way back inside the ship. But the *fog* was too thick. I could not see a thing.

"Help!" I screamed again. "Is there anyone out there?"

No one answered.

LOST AT SEA

Then I heard a shout. It sounded like Captain Nelson. The ship made a loud groaning noise. It sounded like it was trying to stop.

But the ICEBERG was getting closer and closer! I had to warn my family.

I ran across the ship, feeling my way with my paws. Finally, I found a door. I ran inside.

The ship's crew was running around in a panic. I did not see my family anywhere.

"Thea, Benjamin, where are you?" I yelled.

They didn't answer me. Instead, I heard Captain Nelson shout, **"LOWER THE LIFEBOATS!"**

I knew that could not be good!

The next moment, I heard a *terrible* noise. It sounded like two mountains crashing into each other. The ship lurched.

I lost my balance and tumbled across the floor. The ship rocked again. This time, I rolled out of the open door onto the deck.

"*HELP!*" I screamed. I tried to grab on to something. Anything.

Suddenly, a huge **WAVE** crashed over the railing. I struggled against it, but it was no use. The wave carried me off the boat and into the sea!

I gasped. The water was **FREEZING** cold. Then I felt a firm paw on my tail. Someone pulled me out of the water.

"I've got you, Geronimo!" It was Trap! He must have found his way to one of the lifeboats.

Trap pulled me up next to him. I looked around, dazed. We were not on a lifeboat. We were on an **iceberg!** The very same iceberg that had crashed into the ship!

I struggled to my feet, **shivering**. Trap was not alone. Thea, Benjamin, Pinky, and Merry were all on the iceberg. I was happy to see them safe.

But I was not happy for long.

There was no sign of the ship. The **thick fog** did not lift. It wrapped around us like a cold, wet blanket.

"Let's dig a shelter in the ice," Thea suggested. We dug for hours. Then we **huddled** inside, trying to keep warm. But we were still cold. Icicles dripped from my whiskers.

Besides being cold, we were hungry, too. And Trap kept making things worse.

"Wouldn't a **hot cheese** pizza be delicious right now?" he said, licking his snout. "Or maybe a grilled **cheddar** sandwich.

Or a triple-decker creamy cheesecake. Or maybe . . ."

Trap went on and on for hours. I was so hungry, I wanted to eat my socks.

We were lost at sea all night. The next morning, I was shivering and daydreaming about CHEDDAR CHEESE when I heard Benjamin shout.

"Uncle, look! It's a helicopter!"

We crawled out of the shelter. Benjamin was right. A helicopter flew in the distance. The writing on it read *MouseTV*.

As the helicopter got closer, we heard the loud whir of its blades. Then we heard another sound: music.

"It's a ship!" Benjamin cried.

It was a ship—and it was coming to rescue us!

Thea, Pinky, and Merry let out a cheer.

Then they began to dance.

"Dance with us, Boss," Pinky said. "You'll get warm!"

POOR NELSON

Captain Nelson greeted us as we boarded the ship.

"We thought we had lost you," he said. "My crew and I survived the shipwreck. We didn't lose a single rat."

The ship's crew cheered and clapped.

Captain Nelson turned to Thea. He fell to his knees.

"MY DARLING, I HAD LOST ALL HOPE OF EVER SEEING YOU AGAIN!" he said.

Thea giggled. She held out her paw for him to kiss.

"I'm so glad you found us," she said.

I shook my snout. Poor Captain Nelson! I had seen this before. Even the toughest rodent will melt like cream cheese in the sun when my sister is around. It's too bad she is such a heartbreaker!

Oh, my darling!

A MASS OF MEDALS

Thea and Pinky spent all day getting the new ship ready for the New Year's Eve party. It started at ten o'clock. **MouseTV**'s camera mice roamed around, filming everything.

A loud rock band started off the party inside the ship. I went out on deck to get away from the noise.

Captain Nelson walked up to me. He was wearing his dress uniform. It was as white and shiny as a fresh ball of mozzarella. A mass of shiny medals was pinned to his chest.

"HOW IS EVERYTHING GOING, STILTON?" he barked loudly.

"Just fine," I said. I sighed. Is a little peace

and quiet too much to ask for?

Nelson looked around the ship, smoothing his whiskers.

"THIS SHIP IS QUITE NICE," he said. **"NOT AS NICE AS MINE, THOUGH."**

"It must be hard to lose your ship," I remarked.

Captain Nelson shrugged. **"I HAD INSURANCE,"** he said.

Then Thea walked up to us. Captain Nelson's voice suddenly became *as sweet as a cheese lollipop.*

"MY DARLING, YOU LOOK BEAUTIFUL," he said. **"EVEN MORE BEAUTIFUL THAN THE MOON IN THE SKY!"**

"Why, thank you, Captain," Thea said. "You look very smart yourself."

Captain Nelson beamed. **"DO YOU THINK**

SO?" he asked, puffing out his chest. **"I DO HAVE A FEW MEDALS. I GOT THIS ONE FOR SAVING A SUBMARINE DURING THE CHEDDAR WARS. THIS ONE IS FOR BRAVERY IN BATTLE. AND THIS ONE . . ."**

Thea squeaked with delight.

"How fascinating!" she said. "You must tell me everything!"

I groaned. I could not wait for the party to be over!

NEW YEAR'S EVE AT THE NORTH POLE

I could not decide what was worse: Listening to Captain Nelson sweet-talk Thea, or listening to the loud rock band.

I do not like noise.

I do not like loud music.

But above all, I do not like New Year's Eve. Every year, I get dragged to a noisy, crowded party. All I really want to do is to spend a quiet evening at home. I like to curl up in my pawchair, watching a romantic movie and nibbling on cheese crisps.

But I was far from home. I decided to go back inside and see what was happening. Pinky stood close to the band, squeaking, **"LOUDER! LOUDER!"**

Thea and Captain Nelson came in and began to dance. Pinky started dancing with Benjamin. Everyone looked very **happy**.

Then I heard a small voice behind me.

"Happy New Year, Boss."

I turned around. It was Merry. She looked a little bit sad.

"Why aren't you dancing with the others?" I asked.

Merry looked down at the floor. "No one has asked me to dance yet," she squeaked softly.

"Really?" I said. "A *charming* little mouse like you?"

Merry brightened. "Do you really think I'm charming, Boss?" she shrieked. "Really?"

"Of course you are *charming*," I said. "You are very charming . . . but a little too loud at times."

Poor Merry looked so unhappy now. I knew what I had to do.

"May I have this dance?" I asked.

Merry squealed with delight. Then we scurried onto the dance floor.

THE DAWNING OF A NEW DAY

I like to think I am an honest mouse.

So I will be honest with you now.

I was sure I would have a terrible time at the party. I thought the loud music would burst my eardrums. Or that I would sprain my paws dancing. But I had a wonderful time! I really let my fur down.

Merry and Pinky taught me all kinds of dances. We danced to hip-hop and disco music. We swayed to salsa and did the merengue. We even slam-danced to LOUD ROCK MUSIC!

I discovered that potato chips dunked in ketchup are delicious. And that temporary tattoos can look very stylish.

Pinky did want me to get my tail pierced, but I refused. I do have my limits!

The mice from **MouseTV** had organized a tango dance competition: The last couple to leave the dance floor would win. Merry and I entered the contest together. We danced the tango for eight hours straight! In the end,

we were the only mice left standing. We won first prize—a trophy carved out of a block of sharp cheddar! Can you believe that?

The party lasted until the morning. Waiters walked around, handing out **hot chocolate**

and cheese Danish. We all walked out on deck to watch the sunrise.

It was very moving. For me, it felt like the dawn of a new day, a new year . . .

maybe even a new life!

BACK AT THE OFFICE

When we got back home, I felt like a new mouse.

I was no longer the same plain old Geronimo Stilton.

I had changed.

For one thing, I did not feel like listening only to quiet classical music anymore. When I heard a **R O C K** song playing, I found myself humming along with the tune.

For another thing, I found that I did not like my wardrobe anymore. Yes, it was expensive. I had lots of wool suits with gold buttons and cashmere sweaters. But now they did not seem AS FREE AND COMFORTABLE as a simple pair of jeans.

I looked at my closet and frowned. There was a neat row of mouse-gray suits. And a rack of tasteful ties from my aunt Sweetfur. She gave me a new one every Christmas. Last year's tie had tiny 🐾🐾🐾🐾🐾🐾🐾🐾🐾 on it.

But everything looked so boring now. I had to do something. And I knew just the mouse to help me.

I called Pinky. "I need a favor," I said. "Will

you go **clothes shopping**
with me?"

Pinky didn't say anything at first. I
thought I heard her giggle.

"OK, Boss," she finally said. "Give me
ten minutes. And bring plenty of money!"

We shopped until we **dropped** all
afternoon. I bought all kinds of jeans.

*I bought dark blue jeans, faded jeans,
acid-washed jeans, and black jeans.
I bought high-cut, low-cut, boot-cut, and baggy jeans.
I bought jeans with buttons, zippers, and laces.*

But that wasn't all.

With Pinky's help,
*I bought a denim jacket
to match every pair of jeans.
I bought wide belts and skinny belts.
I bought baggy T-shirts and belly shirts.*

THE FINISHING TOUCH

"You are almost perfect, Boss," Pinky said. "You just need one more thing."

Pinky took me to a fancy shop that only sold sunglasses. **Cheese nips!** I had never seen so many pairs of sunglasses in my life. I tried on 103 pairs (I counted).

Pinky gave me her opinion on every pair.

"Not those, Boss. Those make you look like a clown."

"Not those. They make you look like a crook."

"Those make you look silly."

"Those make you look cheesy."

Pinky finally threw up her paws. "I give up!" she shouted. "You are a **hopeless case**, Boss. You've got the wrong snout."

"Wrong snout?" I asked, insulted. "What do you mean?"

The sales clerk walked up to

us. "Yes, you do have a rather unusual snout," she said. "Perhaps our sunglasses are not for you. You are a bit old for them."

Ouch! That comment hurt. But Pinky did not give up.

"Try these, Boss!" she squeaked. "I think I found the *perfect pair* for you."

I looked in the mirror. They were perfect!

I could not wait to show off the new me!

"I found the perfect pair for you."

TURNING OVER A NEW LEAF

Mousella did not recognize me when I came into the office the next morning.

"Mr. Stilton?" she asked, puzzled. "ARE YOU GOING TO A COSTUME PARTY?"

I ignored her comment. I opened my office door and began to squeak loudly.

"Everything here has got to change!" I shouted. "I need new furniture. No more boring wood. Maybe steel, or glass . . . no, plastic! In bright colors to match the walls. Red, orange, purple, yellow, and pink. Yes, pink!"

I walked around the office, measuring and planning. "In that corner, I want a soda-and-snack machine. And a wide-screen TV with a video game player over there."

Mousella scribbled notes onto a pad. "Yes, Mr. Stilton," she said quickly. "I'll arrange everything."

She started to walk away. "I'm not done yet!" I shouted after her. "I want a stereo. An **enormouse** one! With giant speakers. I want to make my eardrums vibrate!"

Fur Kids Only

I left my office and walked up to the next floor. I knocked on the door marked

Fur Kids Only

I could hear squeaks and giggles coming from inside. The door opened, and I stepped in.

The room had walls streaked with bright colors and five or six desks covered in stacks of papers. All of the computers had animated screen savers: flying chunks of cheese, screaming rock singers, and whirling colors. A fur-raising rock song **blared** from the stereo. It was Fuzzy Fuzzborn's latest hit! I could not help myself. I started dancing on the spot.

Pinky waved at me and turned down the volume. "Hi there, Boss!" she squeaked.

Merry and the other young mice on the staff ran up to me. They all had a copy of a magazine in their paws.

"This is the new issue of **Fur Kids Only**," Merry said proudly. "Look, Fuzzy Fuzzborn's on the cover. You haven't forgotten about the concert tonight, have you?"

"Of course not!" I said happily. "I picked out an outfit to wear this morning. I've got a T-shirt with Fuzzy's face on it."

Pinky smiled. "You **rock**, Boss!" she said. "You used to be so boring.

Always with your fur in a frazzle. But you've really loosened up. Good for you!"

Dear Boss . . .

This morning I got this e-mail:

Hiya Boss,

It's Pinky and Merry here at the keyboard. We're using our mouse, of course! :-)

Our mission is accomplished! You are a brand-new mouse.

You have a new wardrobe. A new life. No girlfriend yet, but we are not miracle workers, Boss. LOL!

And we both have something we have always wanted: our own magazine!

We are fourteen. And we rule the world! What could be better than that?

By the way, we still need to talk about our payment—or should we say, our RAISE. There are two of us, after all. Wait until you get our bill. Your fur will probably turn white with shock!

Speaking of white fur, we thought we should tell you that even though you are pretty cool, you are still old. Maybe you should take up a nice quiet hobby, like collecting cheese rinds.

TTFN,
Pinky and Merry

Many readers ask us where we work . . .

These are the busy streets of New Mouse City.

This is the headquarters of The Rodent's Gazette.

And finally, these are the offices of

Fur Kids Only.

ABOUT THE AUTHOR

Born in New Mouse City, Mouse Island, Geronimo Stilton is Rattus Emeritus of Mousomorphic Literature and of Neo-Ratonic Comparative Philosophy. For the past twenty years, he has been running *The Rodent's Gazette*, New Mouse City's most widely read daily newspaper.

Stilton was awarded the Ratitzer Prize for his scoop on *The Curse of the Cheese Pyramid*. He has also received the Andersen 2000 Prize for Personality of the Year. One of his bestsellers won the 2002 eBook Award for world's best ratlings' electronic book. His works have been published all over the globe.

In his spare time, Mr. Stilton collects antique cheese rinds and plays golf. But what he most enjoys is telling stories to his nephew Benjamin.

Want to read my next adventure?
It's sure to be a fur-raising experience!

SURF'S UP, GERONIMO!

Blue skies, sandy beaches . . . I was dreaming of a nice, quiet vacation in the sun. I needed to get away from the rat race for a while. And without Thea and Trap to drag me on some crazy adventure, I'd be able to relax for once. But instead of a beautiful seaside resort, I found myself staying at a fleabag hotel that was falling down around my ears! Oh, would I ever be able to enjoy my vacation?

Don't miss any of my other fabumouse adventures!

#1 Lost Treasure of the Emerald Eye

#2 The Curse of the Cheese Pyramid

#3 Cat and Mouse in a Haunted House

#4 I'm Too Fond of My Fur!

#5 Four Mice Deep in the Jungle

#6 Paws Off, Cheddarface!

#7 Red Pizzas for a Blue Count

#8 Attack of the Bandit Cats

A Fabumouse
~~ion for Geronimo

#10 All Because of a
Cup of Coffee

#11 It's Halloween,
You 'Fraidy Mouse!

#12 Merry Christmas,
Geronimo!

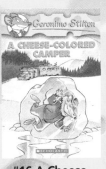

The Phantom of
he Subway

#14 The Temple of
the Ruby of Fire

#15 The Mona
Mousa Code

#16 A Cheese-
Colored Camper

7 Watch Your
iskers, Stilton

#18 Shipwreck on
the Pirate Islands

and coming soon

#20 Surf's Up,
Geronimo!

Geronimo's

Joke Contest

Do you like telling your friends jokes that make them squeak? So do I! And I'm always looking for new jokes. Send me a few of your favorites, and I'll send you a fun gift. If you make me laugh out loud, your joke may appear in one of my future bestsellers!

Send your **JOKE** along with your name, mailing address, city, state, zip code, and birthday to me at the following address:

Thundering Cattails, I Want to Make
Geronimo Stilton Laugh Out Loud!
c/o Scholastic Inc.
557 Broadway
Box 711
New York, NY 10012

THE RODENT'S GAZETTE

1. Main Entrance
2. Printing presses (where the books and newspaper are printed)
3. Accounts department
4. Editorial room (where the editors, illustrators, and designers work)
5. Geronimo Stilton's office
6. Storage space for Geronimo's books

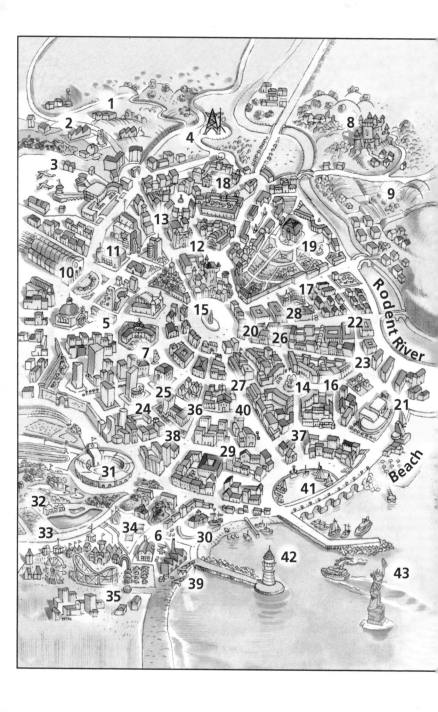

Map of New Mouse City

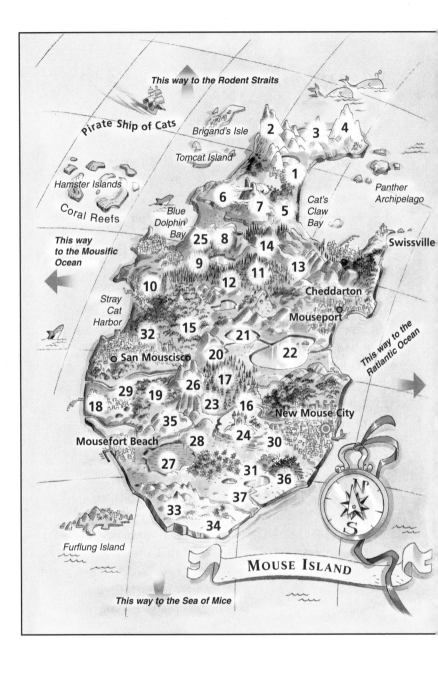

Map of Mouse Island

1. Big Ice Lake
2. Frozen Fur Peak
3. Slipperyslopes Glacier
4. Coldcreeps Peak
5. Ratzikistan
6. Transratania
7. Mount Vamp
8. Roastedrat Volcano
9. Brimstone Lake
10. Poopedcat Pass
11. Stinko Peak
12. Dark Forest
13. Vain Vampires Valley
14. Goose Bumps Gorge
15. The Shadow Line Pass
16. Penny Pincher Lodge
17. Nature Reserve Park
18. Las Ratayas Marinas
19. Fossil Forest
20. Lake Lake
21. Lake Lake Lake
22. Lake Lakelakelake
23. Cheddar Crag
24. Cannycat Castle
25. Valley of the Giant Sequoia
26. Cheddar Springs
27. Sulfurous Swamp
28. Old Reliable Geyser
29. Vole Vail
30. Ravingrat Ravine
31. Gnat Marshes
32. Munster Highlands
33. Mousehara Desert
34. Oasis of the Sweaty Camel
35. Cabbagehead Hill
36. Rattytrap Jungle
37. Rio Mosquito

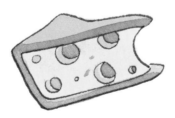

Dear mouse friends,
Thanks for reading, and farewell
till the next book.
It'll be another whisker-licking-good
adventure, and that's a promise!

Geronimo Stilton